The Chair is Too High

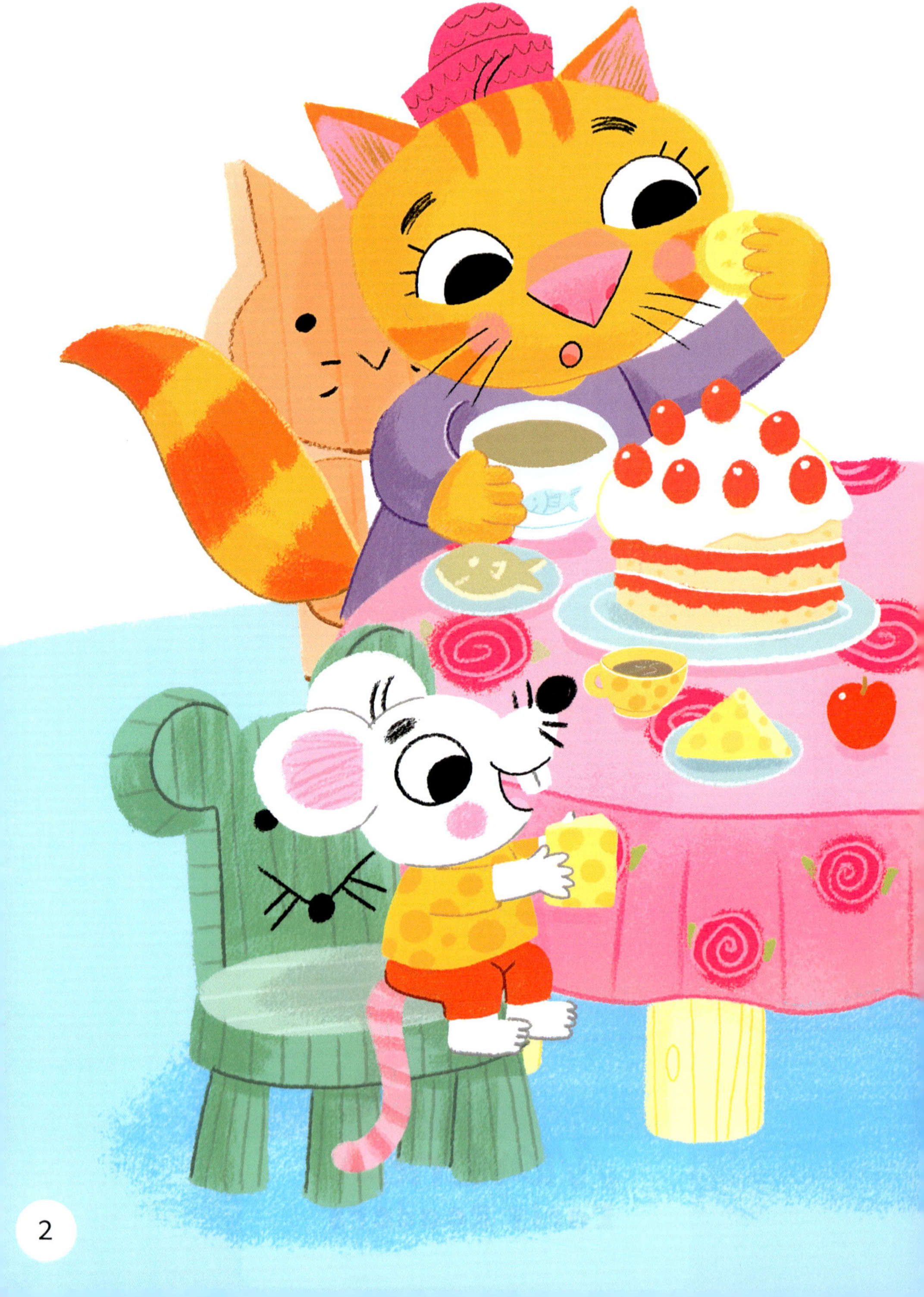

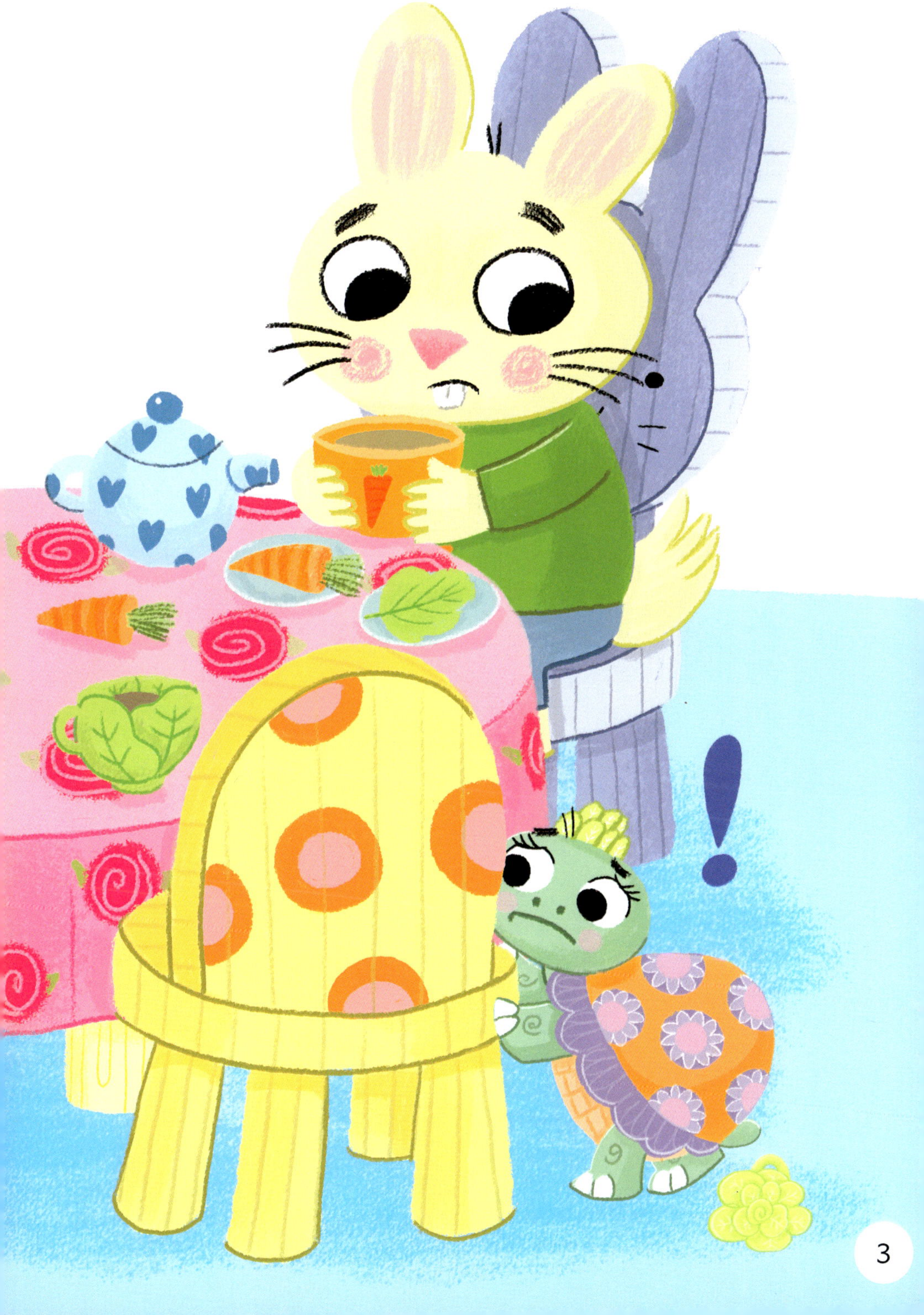

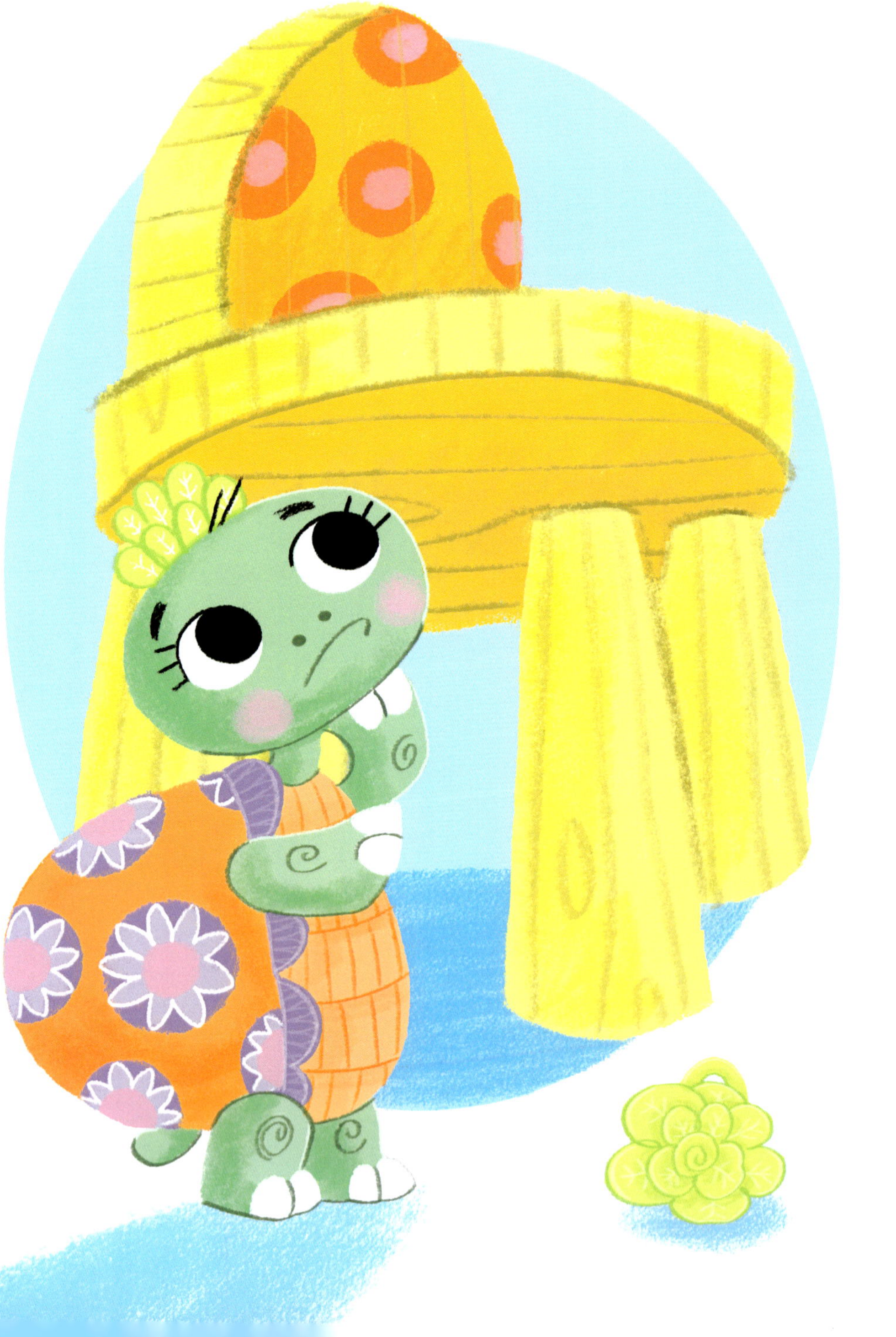

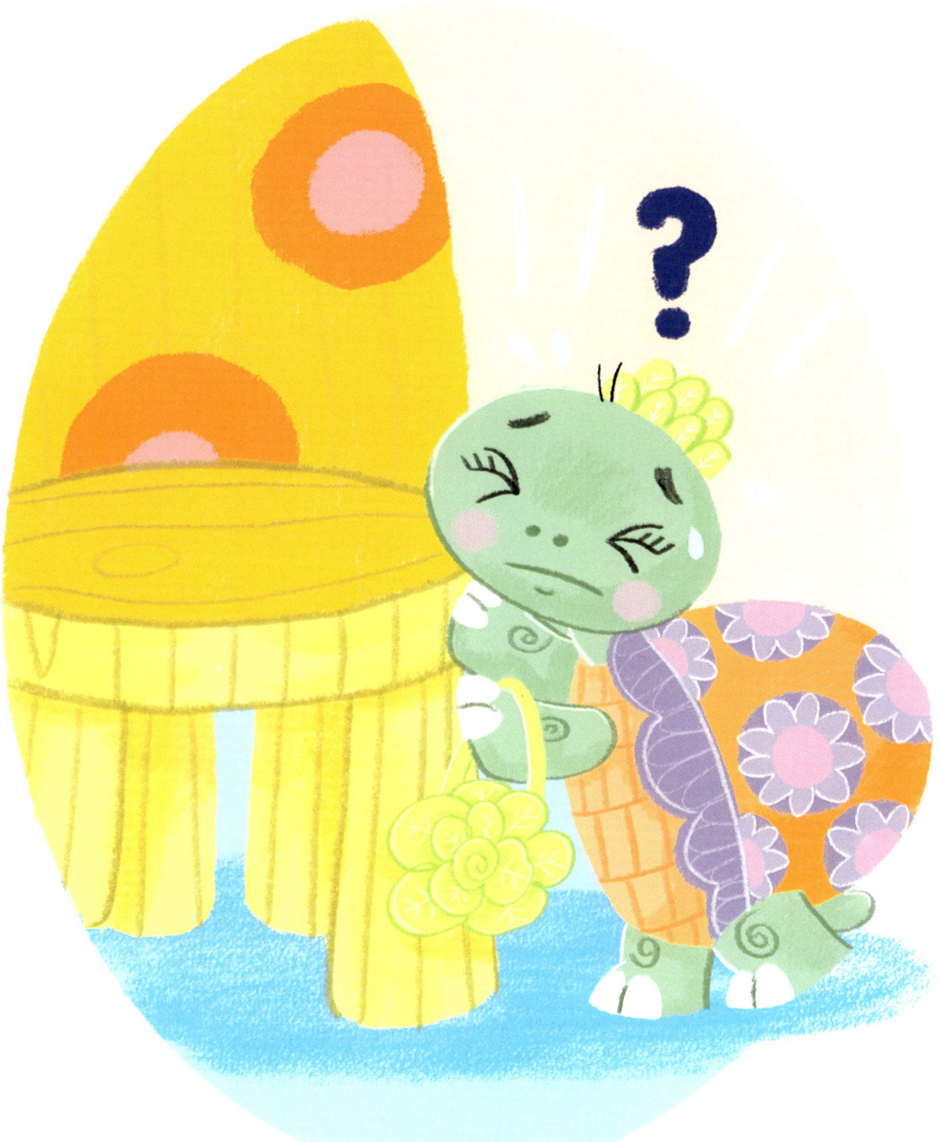

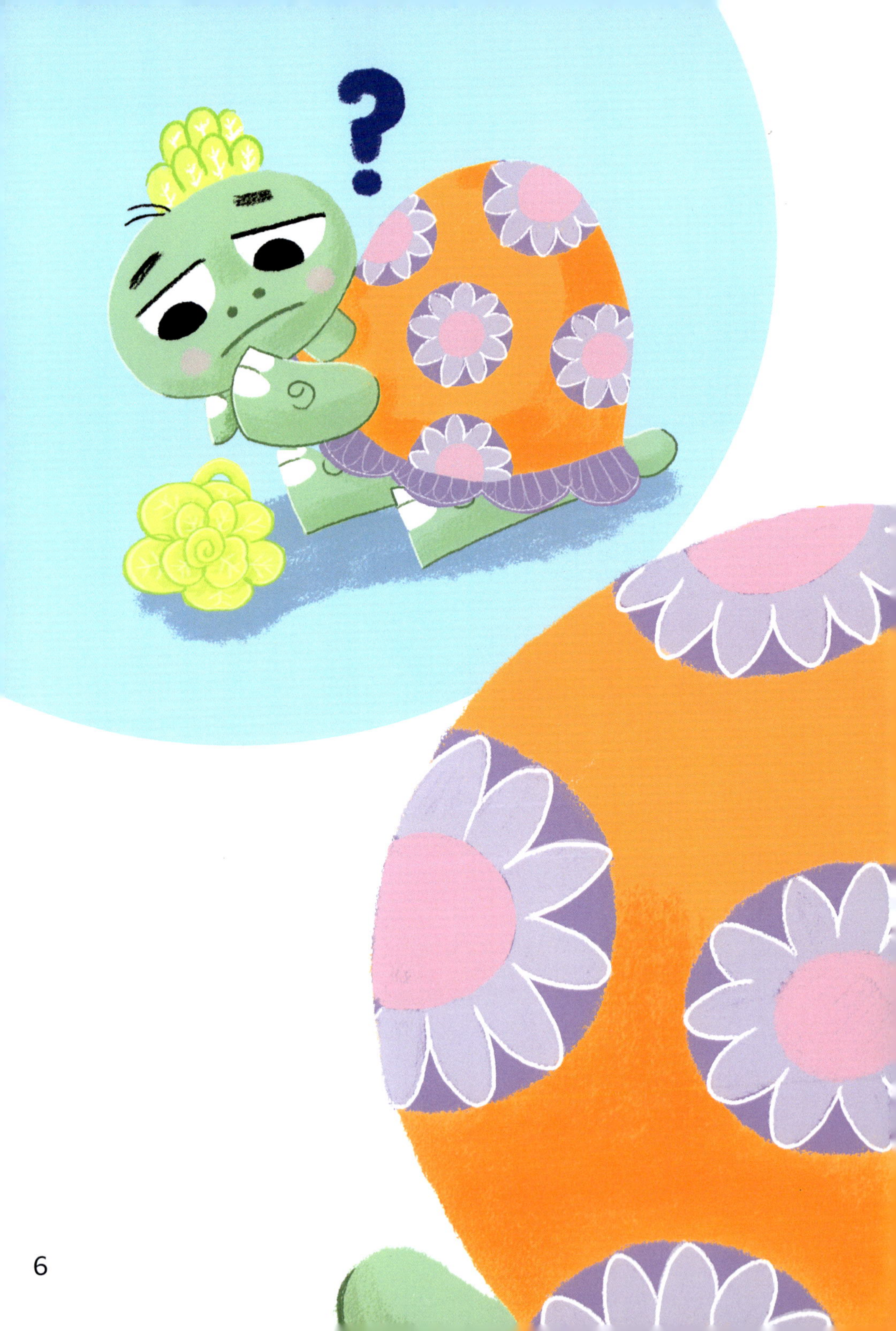

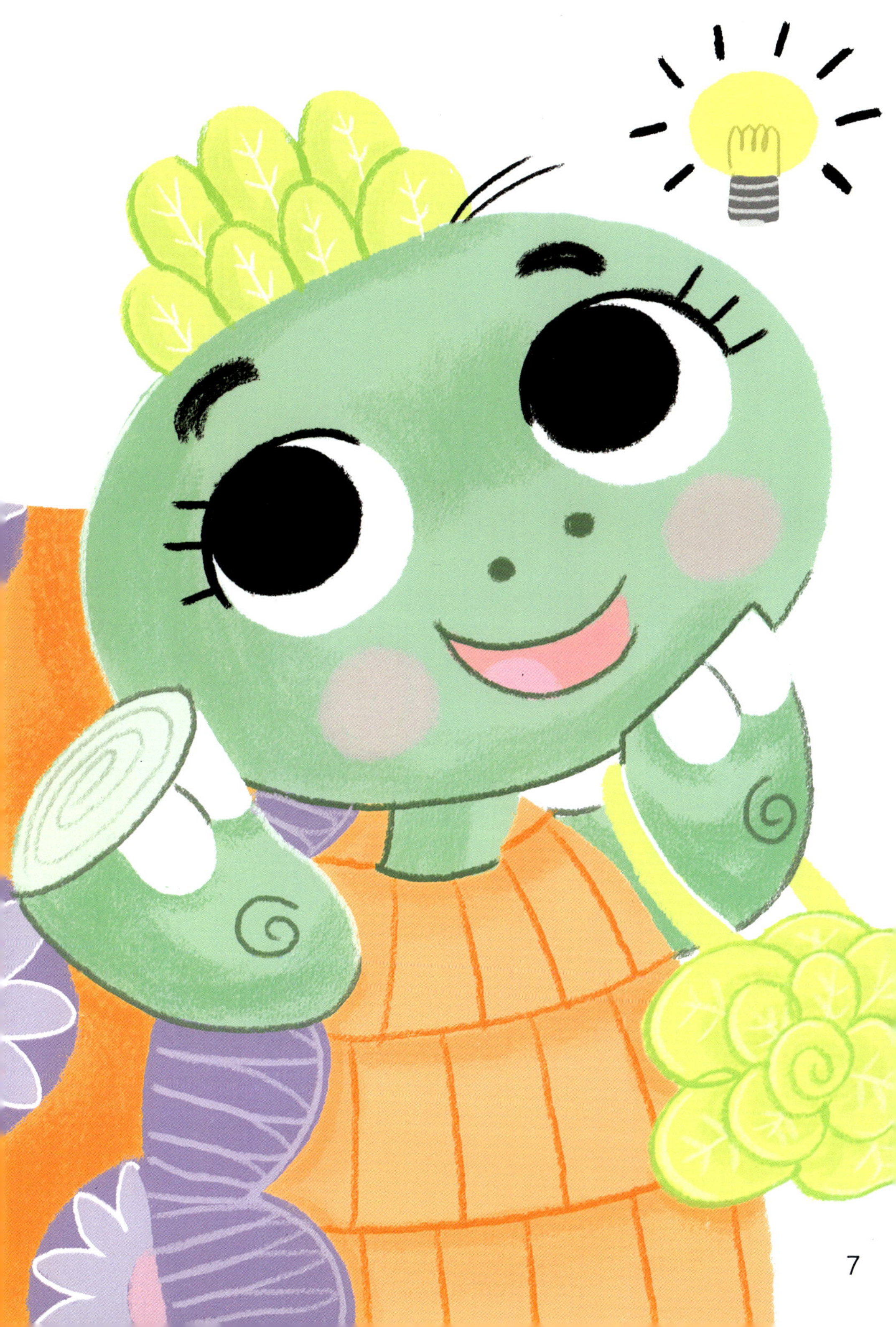

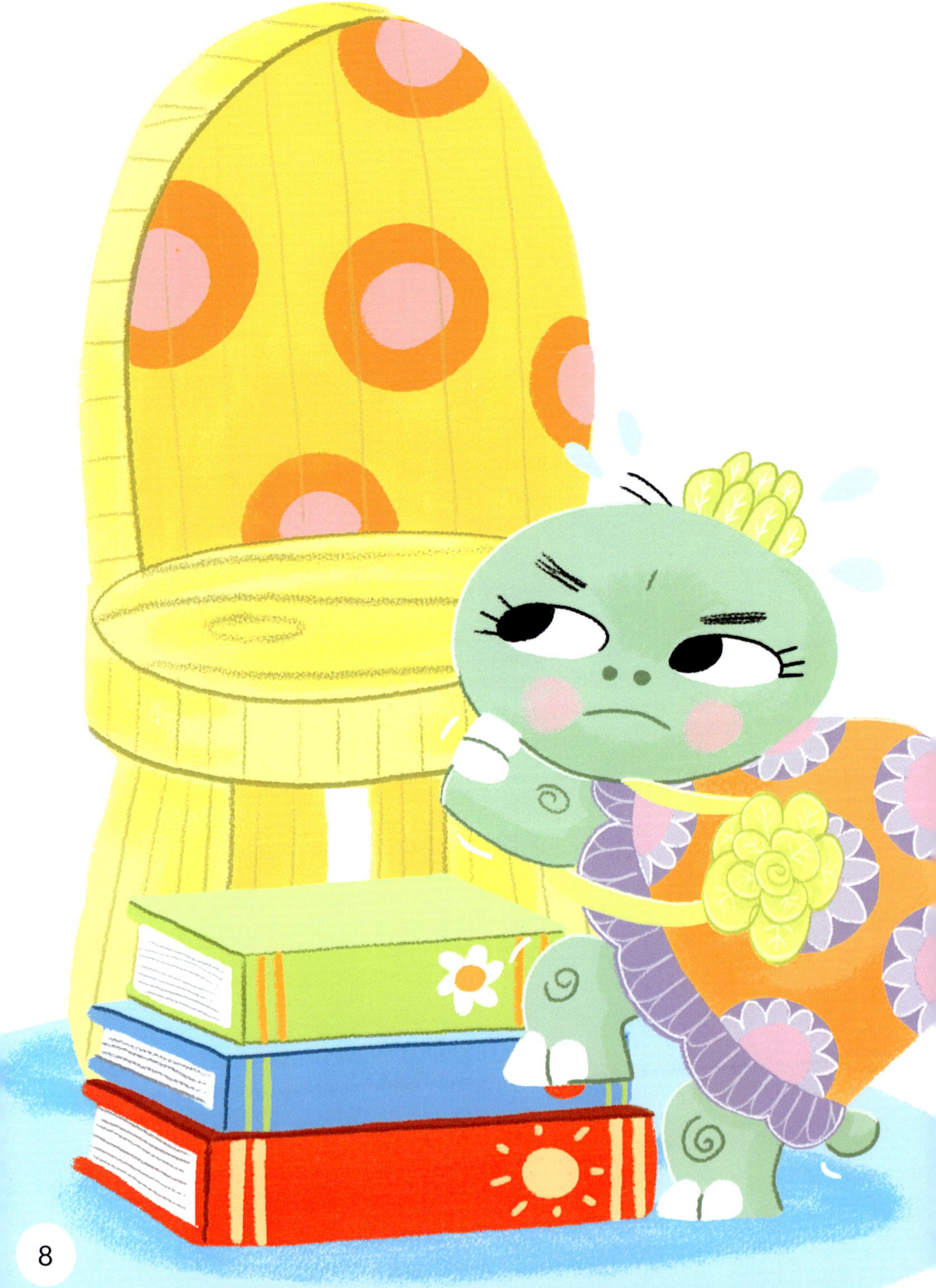

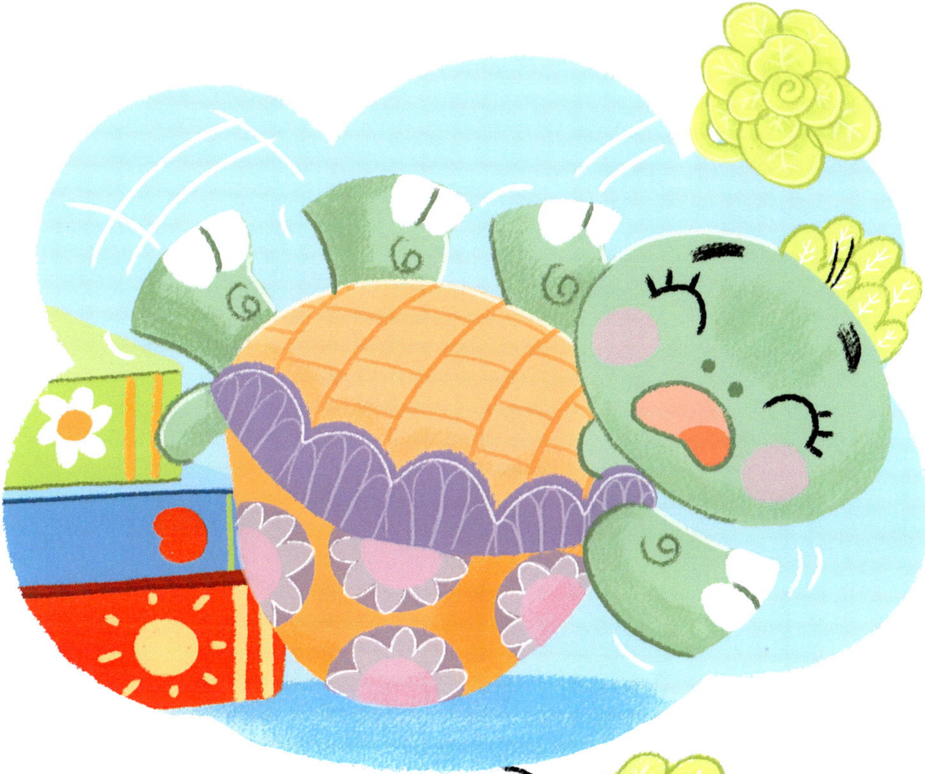

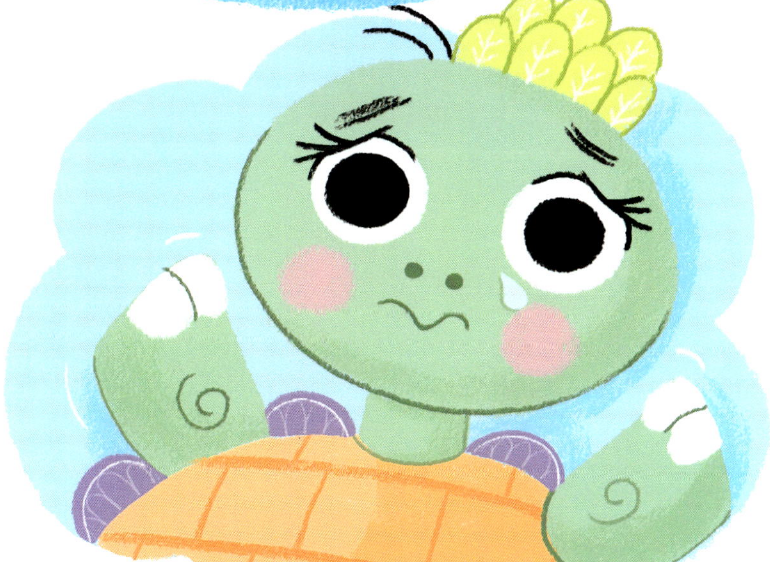

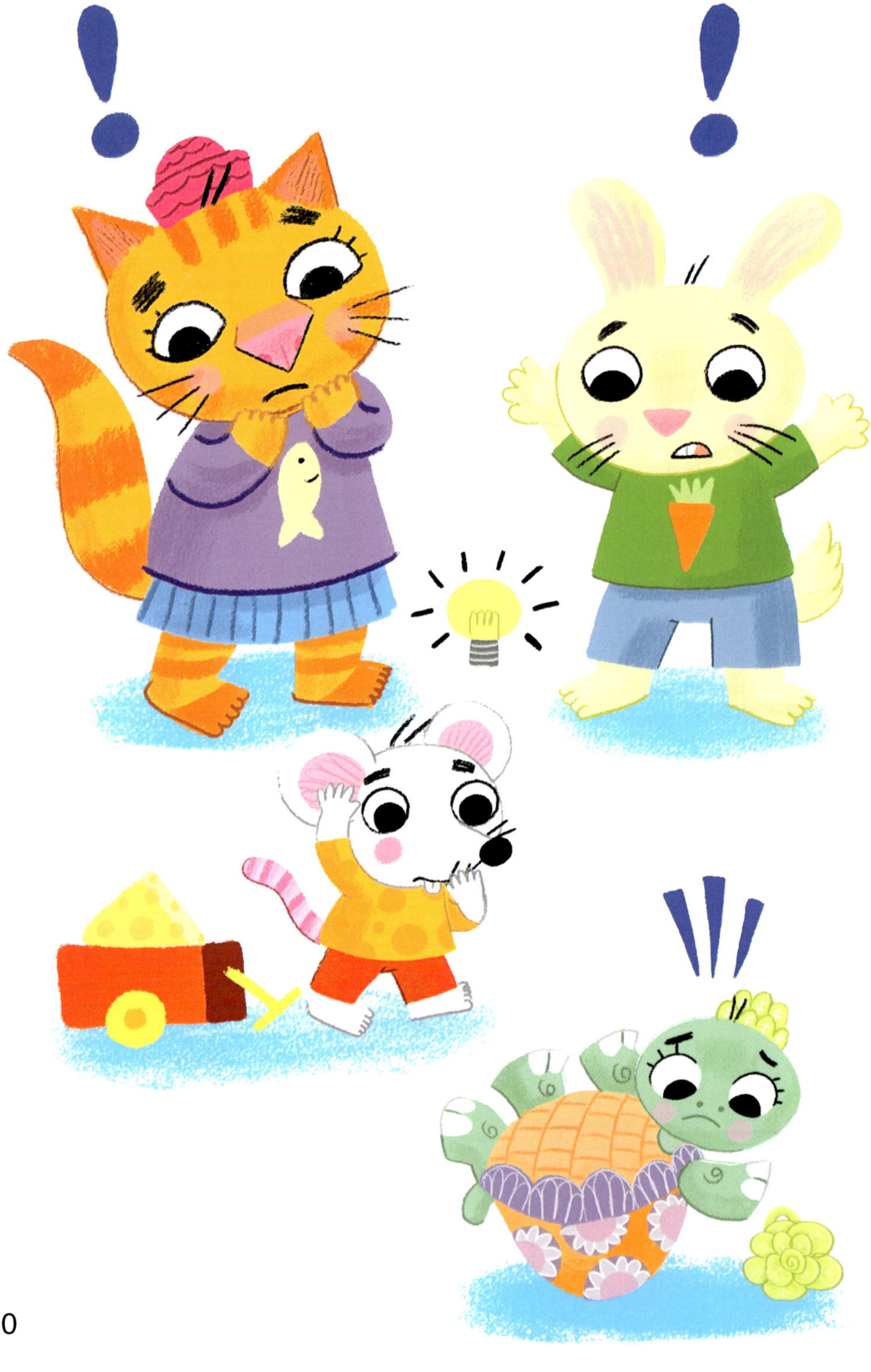

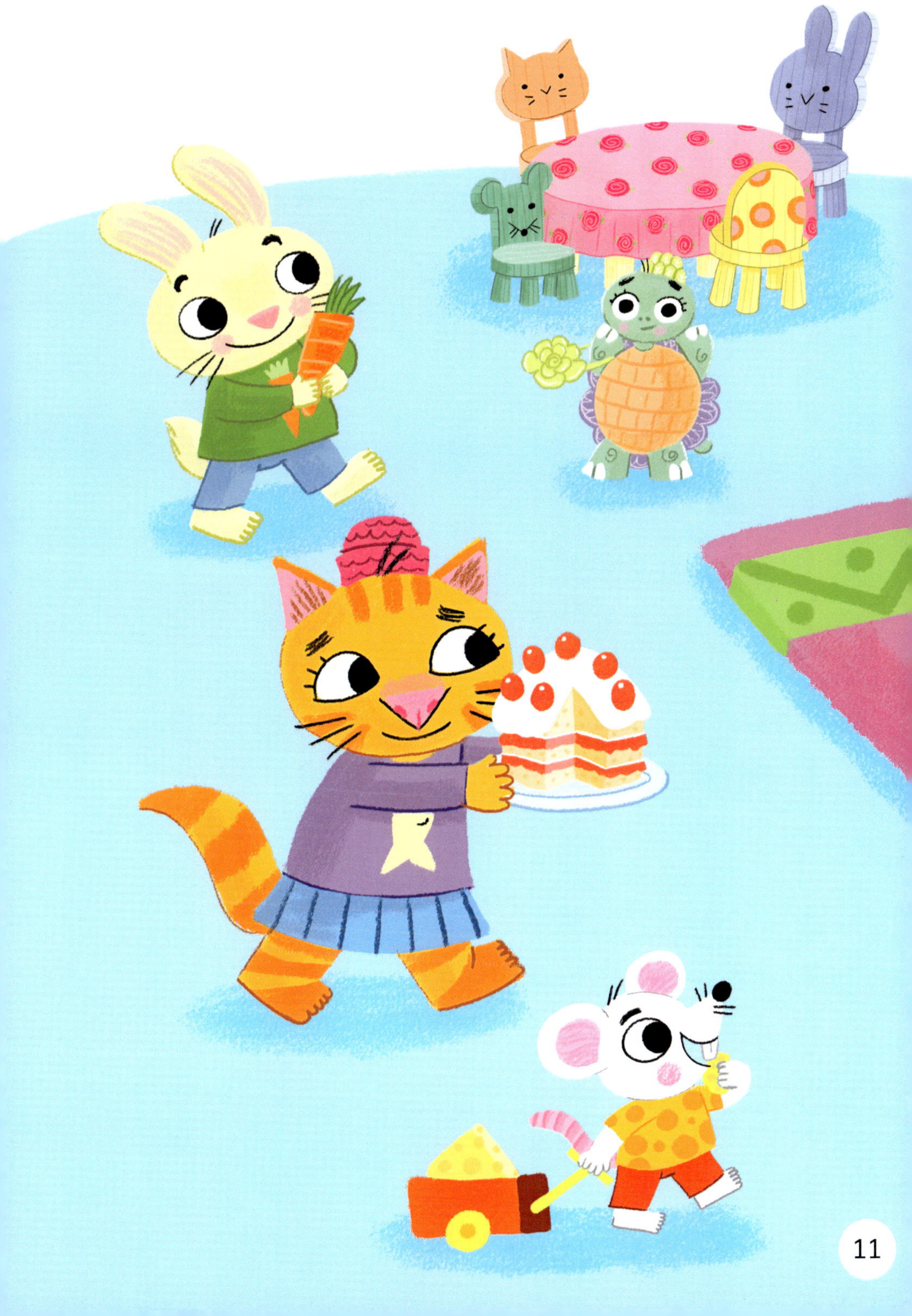

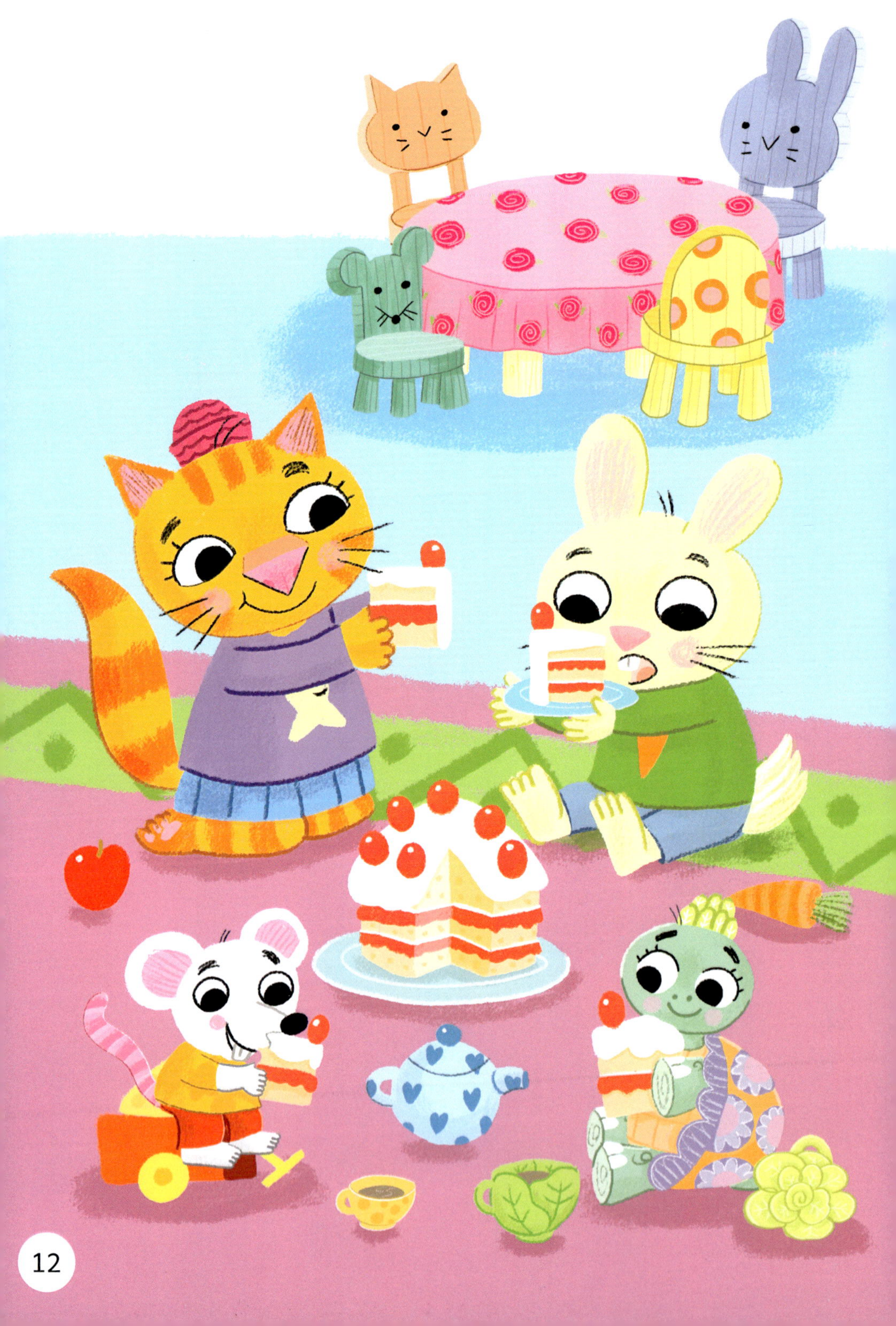